A message in code starts Tim off on an exciting treasure hunt through a dark cave, an underground tunnel, and other strange places until at the end he finds a happy surprise.

As in all Eric Carle's books, there is more to this than the fun of the story. Pattern recognition, matching shapes, following instructions, and simple map reading are introduced.

But Eric Carle has designed this book primarily to provide real pleasure for very young children. His boldly colorful illustrations, the simple but suspenseful story, and the joyful surprise of the ending amply fulfill this goal.

For Bill Martin

The Secret Birthday Message
By Eric Carle

HarperCollins*Publishers*

On the night before Tim's birthday he found a strange envelope under his pillow. He sat up straight in his bed and opened the letter. Inside was a Secret Message!

And this is what it said:

WHEN THE ⬤ COMES UP

LOOK FOR THE BIGGEST ★.

BELOW IT YOU'LL SEE A ⬯.

BEHIND THAT IS THE ▲. GO IN.

LOOK UP TO FIND A ⬤. CRAWL THROUGH.

GO DOWN ⬓

WALK STRAIGHT AHEAD TO A ▮. OPEN IT.

YOU WILL SEE A ▬ CLIMB UP AND THROUGH.

THAT'S WHERE YOU'LL FIND YOUR BIRTHDAY GIFT!

HAPPY BIRTHDAY!

When the moon comes up

Look for the biggest star.

Below it you'll see a rock.

Look up to find a round opening. Crawl through.

at is the ent

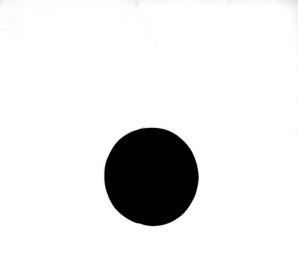

Go down the stairs.

Walk straight ahead to a door. Open it.

You will see an opening. Climb up and through.

That's where you'll find your birthday gift!

(Can you find your way back? See the next page!)

ERIC CARLE, internationally known author and illustrator, believes that children really enjoy learning, and his award-winning picture books reflect this conviction. Filled with color and humor, each of his strikingly designed books brings the child a happy lesson in counting, or reading, or provides a pleasant introduction to the days of the week, the seasons, or other basic concepts.

Born in the United States, Mr. Carle spent his early years in Germany, and studied at the Akademie der bildenden Künste in Stuttgart. His books have been published in Japan, England, and many countries in Europe, as well as in the United States, and one of them was chosen the best picture book at the International Children's Book Fair in 1970. *Do You Want to Be My Friend?*, published in 1971, was an Honor Book in *Book World*'s Children's Spring Festival.

Published in West Germany, 1971,
and in the United States of America,
Canada, and the United Kingdom, 1972.
This work is protected
internationally in countries that
are members of the Berne Union.
All rights reserved. Printed in Singapore.
First Miniature Edition, 1991
ISBN 0-06-020102-9
LC Number 91-8306
E